The Bridges
of Chara

an allegory of your brain's emotional
landscape

Denesia Christine Huttula

The Bridges of Chara: **an allegory of your brain's emotional landscape**
by Denesia Christine Huttula

Cover Image and Design: Joseph Huffman
Interior Illustrations: Joseph Huffman
Publisher: Denesia Christine Huttula
Editor: Pauline Kirke

ISBN-13: 978-1517523428
ISBN-10: 1517523427

Order from Amazon or www.theopenbench.com

Endorsements

"While reading this allegory on Spirit and science I immediately thought of homes where conflict is high and joy is low, where communication is failing but a story would be heard. Complex truth is easily absorbed in a captivating story even by those who are not always ready to listen. Deni has used her experience with these low joy places to write a story that crosses bridges and builds bridges where there were none. On top of that, this is great reading for high joy people as well. Instead of being dragged through the deep waters we soar in hope and understanding of how the brain and spirit work inside and in relationships."

~Dr. Jim Wilder, PhD.
Psychologist with thirty years of clinical experience
Author of several books including *Living From the Heart Jesus Gave You, The Complete Guide to Living with Men,* and *Joy Starts Here.*

"I read the book last week and could not put it down. It's a short read but oh so powerful. So powerful that I immediately took some of the experiences in the story and related them to my family. I decided to create a joy (Chara) experience with my youngest daughter. At dinner, she expressed she wanted to go on a bike ride later. I'm sure in her mind it wasn't going to happen but then after cleaning up dinner, I asked her if she still wanted to go. Of course she said yes.

As we ventured out on our bike ride, the story was playing in my mind. I was appreciating the surroundings with the sun setting and grateful for the time with my teenager. As we came around corner, approaching our home, a beautiful young deer was grazing in our front yard. We both paused and took it in. As we hopped back onto our bikes I told my daughter that I appreciated this time with her and if she hadn't suggested it we would have not had that experience together. She immediately looked back at me and our eyes connected. She had a huge smile on her face and I knew she had been on Chara Island."

~ Michelle D. Howe
Leadership Coach, Author of *It is Finished*

"As an occupational therapist who is an old hand now in the world of inner healing and recovery, I am excited for how Denesia Huttula has compressed years of learning into one succinct, palatable, and powerful short story! To read it is to be positively changed!"

Joan T. Warren
MHS, OTR/L

Dedication & Appreciation

❖ To my mother, Joan - my first bridge master. Thank-you for giving to me, everything you had. I really appreciate all that you did, and still do for me. I'm glad to be with you, and glad to continue building bridges with you for many more years to come.

❖ To my dad, Ed and my other mom, Maritza - my tour guides! Thank-you for introducing me to everything I know about the brain, emotions, and JOY. I appreciate how you've been such a good example of "how to repair" damaged, weak, or broken bridges. Your joy and tenderness have taught me so much more than all the books on the brain I could possibly read. And Dad, thank-you for planting the seed that became this book!

❖ To my children, Robert and Megan- my unending sources of joy. Every memory we share, on Joy Island, and building bridges back and forth from every emotion, is forever stored in my heart as appreciation memories. I'll never tire of helping you build bridges.

❖ To my husband, Johnny- my bridge maintenance man! Thank-you for being glad to be with me. I couldn't have maintained this life of joy without you. Back and forth we go until our last day.

TABLE OF CONTENTS

Note from the Author

I always grin a little when someone says to me, "It's not brain science", because in this case, it is.

Brain science is a complex yet amazing thing to study. We have much to learn about how our brain works, and the advances in science in this area have not only been incredibly interesting, but incredibly helpful. Understanding how our brains work, and the way they are "wired" is crucial to effecting change in our lives. As a Christian, I am even more encouraged to look at this because it's showing me the blueprint for how God designed my brain to work. Since I believe He knew what He was doing, I have full confidence that there is a reason why He made our brains work the way they do.

Even if you aren't a Christian or a believer in God as our creator, understanding the science of how your brain works will still affect you!

This story was actually first conceived a few years ago while working at a Statewide Inpatient Psychiatric Program for children. I was an assistant teacher there and was tasked with the afternoon "social skills" lessons among many other things. This gave me the opportunity to teach the kids in my class all about their emotions. These children all had extreme difficulty with processing emotions. They were all in this program for varying reasons including, RAD, severe ADHD, schizophrenia, bipolar disorder, and many other psychiatric issues. These kids were all abused, and many were tossed around inside the foster care system for much of their lives. My classroom contained ages 5-17 and as you can imagine, pretty much experienced negative emotional outbursts on a regular basis.

At one point, things were getting stressful and all the teachers and staff were running out of capacity for dealing with all the intensity this particular group of hurting kids was experiencing. I remember crying out to the Lord and wondering if it was even possible to help them.

Then I had an idea. A unique idea for helping "my kids" understand what was going on inside them! I created a lesson and art project that involved our emotions appearing as islands. I created a short story about a magical land where people lived on Joy Island and traveled back and forth to islands with names like: Anger, Fear, Sadness, Shame, Disgust, and Hopeless Despair.

The kids responded with some major lightbulb moments! They totally "got" it and were able to show me exactly what their bridges back to joy looked like in an art project. From that point on they had a language for what was happening to them when they were "stuck in anger" or lacking a bridge back from sadness.

Over the next few months that I worked there, classroom emotional outbursts decreased dramatically; it was amazing how the kids were able to connect with me in joy when they realized I was glad to be with them even when they were experiencing a negative emotion.

Fast forward a few years- and THIS is the basis for this book!

In this more grown of version of the "Joy Island" allegory, you will also have the opportunity to have your own "lightbulb moments".

You may be thinking, "I thought this was a book about "The Bridges to Chara", well, in case you didn't know Chara means Joy in Greek. I chose to use the Greek words for the names of the emotions, as well as for some other very important words in this book. I've included their definitions and pronunciations in the glossary at the back of the book. I'm also including a bookmark on the last page that "translates" all the Greek for you as a handy guide. You can't use the

"It's too hard it's all brain science" OR the "It's all Greek to me" excuse with this book! ☺

If you're interested in all the technical brain development research and discussion, I encourage you to review Appendix E and then follow up with these books:

- *Affect Regulation and the Origin of the Self, Affect Dysregulation and Disorders of the Self, & Affect Regulation and the Repair of the Self* by Dr. Allan Schore
- *The Developing Mind* by Daniel Siegel
- *No-Drama Discipline: The Whole-Brain Way to Calm the Chaos and Nurture Your Child's Developing Mind* by Daniel Siegel and Tina Payne Bryson.
- *Brain-Based Parenting -The neuroscience of caregiving for healthy attachment* by Daniel A. Hughes and Jonathan Baylin
- *Outsmarting Yourself- Catching Your Past Invading the Present and What to do About It* by Dr. Karl Lehman
- *Joy Starts Here: the transformation zone* by E. James Wilder, Edward M. Khouri, Chris M. Coursey and Shelia D. Sutton
- *The Life Model: Living From the Heart Jesus Gave You* by James Friesen, E James Wilder, Anne Bierling, Rick Koepcke and Maribeth Poole.

At the end of each chapter, I have included discussion questions for you to use as part of a small group or along with personal coaching. These questions don't have right or wrong answers. Their purpose is to get you thinking about your experiences and your life. Feel free to either answer them aloud in a group format or write down your answers throughout the week to keep a journal of your process. One of these chapters will include the original "art project" I assigned the children in my class years ago!

It is my hope that as you read this book you will become more self-aware of how your brain handles emotions, just as my "kids" did. However, knowing how you handle them is not enough to restore your brain to its original design. Most likely, your brain has made its own pathways that are inefficient and painful. It is important that you begin exploring emotional and relational exercises to build new pathways in your brain. You will learn about a few of these tools that are helpful in "returning to joy" while you are reading this story and be encouraged to begin using them in the discussion questions.

As a Life and Recovery Coach, I'd be happy to teach you and practice with you during my private coaching sessions. For more information visit www.theopenbench.com.

"BUT I WILL NOT TELL YOU HOW LONG OR HOW SHORT THE WAY WILL BE; ONLY THAT IT LIES ACROSS A RIVER. BUT DO NOT FEAR THAT, FOR I AM THE GREAT BRIDGE BUILDER." ~ASLAN
~C.S. LEWIS

CHAPTER 1

CHARA

Whether you start the story with "Once upon a time" or "In the beginning" you'll discover a place where everything is just as it should be.

With her eyes closed, she could feel the sun shining warmly on her face. The sweet, soft ocean breeze cooled her skin before she could even think about the heat.

"This must be paradise," she thought, as she wiggled her toes in the white sand beneath her. Eden opened her eyes and gazed around as if waking from a dream. But this was no dream. This was her home now. This island was her home. She belonged here; she could feel it in every cell of her body.

It wasn't always that way though. In fact, she was still new to this beautiful island called Chara (Car-uh). The natives here had told her that Chara means joy, and everyone seemed to agree - it's a joy to live here.

Before she could start thinking about her past, a young woman she had never met before, called out to her, beckoning her over to join them for lunch up in the shade. Realizing that her stomach was beginning to growl, she decided to accept her offer. She soon found herself at a picnic table surrounded by smiling faces. Over a buffet of dishes that smelled just as wonderful as the flowers spilling from Mason jars on the table, Eden was captivated by the way that people here enjoyed one another's company.

There was something magical about the way their faces would light up as they spoke. Their eyes would dance and shine as they looked at each other, and laughter often punctuated their conversation.

This luncheon on the beach felt like a celebration. In a way, she guessed it was. They were celebrating each other. They all seemed so glad to be together. As she ate her meal, she felt nourished deep inside by something other than food.

Sitting opposite her, she noticed a man with wavy gray hair, probably in his 60's, who seemed to be staring at her. He reached across the table and took her hand in his. He looked deep into her eyes and with a grin asked, "Do you want to know our island secret?"

Ordinarily this gesture would have made her extremely uncomfortable, but reassured by the warmth in his eyes and the smiles growing all around the table she surprised herself by answering, "Yes please!"

"My name is Paul, and this is my wife, Mary."

Taking his hand from hers, he put his arm around Mary. Mary's face wore the gentlest smile and it seemed to shoot peace like an arrow, right into Eden's heart.

"Relationship is our secret. We cherish our relationships above anything else on Chara. Even when we have problems and disagreements about other things, we can always find rest in the KNOWING that there's nothing more important to us than each other."

With a wink, he went on, "Relationship is even more important than being the 'right' one in an argument!"

His wife's gentle smile burst into laughter that rippled contagiously among the group so quickly that even Eden joined in.

"In all seriousness," he continued, "our secret is that we are genuinely glad to be with each other. And right now, we are glad to be with YOU! We want to teach you how to live like this too, so that you can truly feel the joy that is Chara."

It occurred to Eden right at that moment that *THIS* feeling was utterly foreign to her. They are "glad to be with me" even though I have done nothing at all to show them I'm a nice person. Their "glad to be with me" shines in their eyes and is written on their faces. It was almost as if joy was a pheromone, released by their mere presence! Could this really be the joy she'd longed for her whole life? Starting to feel a little choked up, she quickly looked down at her plate and managed to whisper, "I'd like that."

Everyone around the table noticed that she couldn't look up at Paul when she answered him. Even though she didn't know what they were doing at the time, they intuitively moved onto a story about something they all remembered, allowing her to swallow the lump in her throat and fend off the tears that unexpectedly threatened to fall. The rest of the meal flowed like a raft down a smooth river. It didn't take long for Eden to rejoin the celebration with everyone else.

After lunch, Eden went on a tour of Chara with Paul and Mary. Chara was thriving! People in Chara had so much respect for each other. It was visible in the marketplace, in the neighborhoods and in their homes.

What struck her most was that people here appeared to honestly know who they were, and even more remarkably, they were all happy being who they were. They didn't seem to expect anyone to be "better" or "different". It was a refreshing, atmosphere changing kind of feeling to realize that no one was comparing themselves to anyone else. Eden had never really considered it before, but these people had such strong identities that there was no room for insecurities or social ladders.

They were especially skillful at knowing and expressing their feelings and needs to each other. Every expression of needs, feelings, or weaknesses, was met with tenderness and care, not judgment. Empathy seemed to be an integral part of every person… all around her- she saw comfort and validation. No one doubted that those around them genuinely cared about them.

As they continued walking around Chara, Eden observed a series of bridges that left the island and connected to other islands. "Where do those go?" she asked.

Paul replied that each person on Chara had their own set of bridges to and from each of the neighboring islands. He explained that this was one of the more enchanting things about Chara.

At the "Marina" Eden found there was so much to learn. It felt like watching a magic show. Paul explained that as you come to the Marina, your very own set of bridges appears.

"These bridges, which are unique to each person, help you get to the islands of Lupe (sorrow/sadness), Orgizo (anger), Phobos (fear), Apalgeo (hopeless despair), Anoia (disgust), and Entrope (shame)."

Feeling confused Eden asked, "Why would anyone ever want to leave Chara to visit those islands? They sound like miserable places!"

"You may be surprised to discover this, but it is sometimes necessary to visit each of those places. In fact, life itself briefly requires us to leave Chara every day. Here, take a look at my bridges; they are strong and stable. Do you see how close they are to Chara? It doesn't take long to get back to Chara across my bridges."

Eden had to admit that the bridges were beautiful to look at. Her curiosity was piqued for sure. This Marina was a mystery she was excited to begin exploring.

Discussion Questions

1. What kind of emotions would you be feeling if you were at a lunch table like the one described in this chapter?

2. Have you ever been overwhelmed with emotion and had people push you to continue talking anyway? How did that feel? (Only a one or two word answer is necessary.)

3. Try to remember a time when someone allowed you to rest when you began to be overwhelmed with emotion. Describe what happened. Try not to spend too much time on what was overwhelming, instead, focus your story on what happened when you were given the chance to rest.

4. What do you think about the idea that "relationships are more important than problems"? Would an outlook like that have an impact on the way you handle conflicts? How?

5. In the story, the island name is Chara, which is the Greek word for joy. How do you think joy relates to the experience of someone being glad to be with you?

6. Think about a time when someone was glad to be with you. Share a story of what was happening. Include how it felt emotionally and physically when you experienced that. Include any details of how you knew they were glad to be with you.

CHAPTER 2

ISLANDS

Even though she was curious about the bridges, Eden still wasn't sure about the idea of ever leaving Chara. It didn't make any sense to her. Why let go of something so wonderful? As her confusion grew, she found herself starting to feel angry.

Before she really knew what was happening, she had slipped across Paul's bridge to Orgizo. Somehow, Paul was already right there with her and assured her that this was only a short visit so he could show her around. The feeling of anger dissipated as she took his hand for safety and began to look at her surroundings.

ANGER

Orgizo was dry and hot. Deeper into the island Eden saw flames and the underbrush smoldered for what looked like miles. A volcano loomed threateningly in the distance. Paul pointed to the beach where embers glowed just beneath the sand for as far as she could see.

"Sometimes things happen to people that were never supposed to happen. The wrong actions of people hurt others and injustice abounds. A trip to Orgizo to get some of these embers can really be what you need to cause you to stop those who hurt others. These potent embers are effective at compelling people to fight for justice, to stand up for themselves, and preventing dangerous predators from attacking. Trips to Orgizo can even be the warning signal you need to realize that someone has wronged you."

"But it's so hot and miserable here. I like it so much better in Chara"

With a smile so wide that most of his teeth showed, Paul answered, "Me too Eden, that's why we aren't meant to live here.... So let's go"

90 seconds later, they had crossed safely back to Chara where Eden felt her body relax. She breathed a deep sigh of relief and felt her skin begin to cool. Her heart rate slowed down and she looked across at Orgizo with new appreciation for its nearby presence.

"Okay, so I think I see now why one might need to go there, but what about the other islands? What about Anoia? I think I could live forever without feeling disgusted." DISGUST

"Let's find out", said Paul, as he started toward another bridge.

This time the bridge was slippery underfoot. Mary was there to help too, and the three of them crossed over. Anoia was green, but not the pretty, lush green you'd expect on a tropical island. This island was rotting. The decomposing leaves resembled old slimy spinach or lettuce leaves left in the fridge for far too long. The pungent smell was so overpowering it caused Eden to gag. Paul handed her a mask and started to explain why such a dreadful place might be important.

"Without access to Anoia, we would have no warning of when something in our path is unhealthy. We need Anoia to send us running from things ...and behaviors... that will make us sick."

"I get it now. Let's get out of here - it doesn't take long at all for me to understand that I am grateful for this warning place!"

Arm in arm, the three of them quickly returned to the mainland where their senses settled.

Eden was starting to realize that there was much more to Chara than she had first been conscious of.

Life on Chara wasn't all roses and perfection. The lives of people on Chara were real. The inhabitants were real people. And the same eyes that sparkled in response to each other continued to sparkle in the midst of real lives that involved crossing bridges to places that were less than optimal places to be.

This understanding was just the tip of the iceberg of truth. But if Eden was going to truly become a member of this new place and call it home, she was going to have to learn about the rest of the neighboring islands.

With a dose of courage welling up inside her, Eden began to walk across Paul's bridge that leads to Phobos. The island itself was covered from shore to shore in dark, deep forest. Though it was nearly noon, the thick, leafy coverage of the trees gave the impression that it was the middle of the night. A chill ran down her spine.

"Paul, I really don't like this place. The urge to leave this island is even more intense than it was on Anoia."

"Phobos isn't supposed to be welcoming and inviting. Its purpose is to make you wish very strongly to get away, to escape from what's chasing you. This dark place compels you to fight, run away, or hide. In their own way, all of these can be effective and can serve to protect you. Without Phobos and the protective reactions of being on Phobos, things that mean to harm you could really hurt you. But be warned, traveling to Phobos for reasons that weren't set out to hurt you is a bad idea. Phobos, like the other islands, is meant to be a temporary place. Once danger has passed you should always return to Chara."

"Sounds good to me, let's get back to Chara now"

But just then, Paul did something unexpected.

Instead of heading for the bridge back to Chara, he stepped onto another bridge that lead from Phobos to another island

"Sometimes the quickest way back to Chara is through Lupe."

SORROW
SADNESS

Lupe was cloudy and muted. A light layer of fog shrouded the entire island. There was a quiet beauty to this foggy island that made Eden feel homesick for a moment. She became more aware of the loss in her life and noticed that her eyes were becoming as moist as the air around her.

Paul placed his arm gently around her shoulders and said, "Lupe is the place to come when you experience a loss. Giving yourself the gift of some time on Lupe gives value to that which you have lost. Lupe is the way we acknowledge and pay respect to that which is no longer or to that which never came to pass."

As both Paul and Mary embraced her, Eden closed her eyes and breathed in the comforting cool air around her. When she opened her eyes she was surprised to find that she was no longer on Lupe, but in fact had instantly returned to Chara with Paul and Mary.

"What? How?"

Mary smiled, "That's the beauty of Lupe. When you are joined by others on Lupe, Chara is just a breath away."

"But what if I had been alone?" asked Eden, trying to make sense of it all.

"The answer to that question is not for today. There is a far side to Lupe that leads to Apalgeo, and this is often where people end up when they have tried and tried to return to Chara on their own without success. But before we go there, let's take a break, and rest here on the shores of Chara."

The three of them sat together on the sand and watched the small waves lapping at their feet for a while. No one said a word. It really was nice just to sit there and rest. In this quiet, safe place, Eden felt peace sink even deeper within her.

Mary broke the silence momentarily, "Did you know Chara also has another name? Chara's second name is Eirene. Eirene is the word for the peaceful rest that comes when we know deep down inside that everything is going to be all right. Eirene is a deep inner peace that often accompanies joy. It's another word for wholeness, or completeness.... The feeling that comes when everything is as it should be." She sighed a long, slow sigh, and then she finished with, "That's what you just felt".

As they continued to sit in silence, Eden started thinking about how nice it was to take some time just to be still. She couldn't remember the last time she had done that - before coming to Chara of course. It occurred to her that it actually seemed like a pretty common and natural occurrence here. She hoped that she would always appreciate it as much as she did now.

She had a sneaking suspicion that she would.

She decided to take this opportunity to thank Paul and Mary for taking her under their wing so to speak. It felt good to be welcomed and encouraged. Telling them how she felt and how much she appreciated them not only felt like a natural thing to do, it invigorated her and gave her the energy and strength to suggest that they visit the remaining islands now.

Soon they were on the next island - a very exposed and barren place. Eden could not see a single tree in sight. For a moment, she felt as if she was naked. Her cheeks flushed and almost instantly, her stomach started to squirm.

SHAME
"Welcome to Entrope." said Mary. "Entrope is no one's favorite place, but it's crucial to our lifestyle on Chara."

Curious to know more, Eden prompted her to explain.

28

"Entrope is like an alarm to us that we've done something that will stop someone from being glad to be with us. If we don't get this warning, we might not realize that our words or actions are damaging the beauty that is Chara. None of us wants to disturb or interrupt the joy that others experience with us. Normally it doesn't take very much to get back to Chara from Entrope, because we care about the people on Chara more than anything. Acknowledging our mistake is a sure way back home from here."

"So, Entrope is like a whistle blower, or like a lifeguard at the swimming pool warning all the kids to stop running?"

"That's one way of looking at it, but I like to think of a trip to Entrope as being more like the gas light in your car. When that light comes on you know you need to stop and fill your tank. If you ignore that light for long, you will end up stranded. The same is true in life. Ignoring the gas light of Entrope and continuing to drive on-insisting that you can keep going no matter what, will eventually leave you alone on the side of the road with no one to help you. Driving on and ignoring the messages that what you're doing is negatively affecting the people around you is a guaranteed way to end up isolated. Getting gas or filling up your tank after a trip to Entrope is as simple as admitting you have made a mistake. Sometimes that is done internally...to yourself or God... and sometimes you need to make amends to the person who was affected by your actions."

Then Paul pointed out that the bridge back to Chara was quite short. He said that returning to Chara was as simple as, "Recognizing that the gas light is on and deciding to pull over soon."

Apparently, you could get off Entrope even before going through the process of admitting your mistakes and making amends. The simple decision to do that was enough to get you back home.

Mary explained some more, "Entrope is a small bare island because it isn't made for lengthy stays. But, as you will learn later, just like all the other islands...it is possible to get stuck there."

"Speaking of getting stuck - there's one more island for us to visit. This island is the farthest away and many people struggle to get there. Apalgeo is on the far side of Lupe and Entrope. Are you ready to explore this island Eden?" said Paul.

HOPELESS DISPAIR

Eden looked across the waterway and saw a small dot in the distance. The bridges to Apalgeo looked complicated. She could see that they extended out from Lupe, Entrope, and even Phobos. She couldn't see anything that connected back to Chara from this last island at all. But she had learned to trust Paul and Mary now, so off they went.

Arriving onto Apalgeo was different from all the other islands. Everything within her seemed to curl up. As a matter of fact, a first glance around this island revealed sleepy little flowers with their petals and leaves all curled up. It was warm and soft everywhere she looked. She had no urge to leave at all. Actually, she found it strangely beautiful and inviting- like it might be a peaceful place to stay for a while. Eden became tired, sleepy, and lost any desire to interact with Paul and Mary. She wandered deeper into Apalgeo and found a spot to lie down.

As she lay down, pain jolted through her body. Those soft, curly flowers that grew everywhere had tiny hidden thorns inside them! Lying on this bed of flowers was sheer torture. As painful as it was, she still had no desire to get up and leave. All she could think about was how heavy she felt and how impossible it would be to find a less painful place. She simply didn't have the energy to move despite the excruciating pain.

Something inside of her shouted like a distant memory, "You can't get up by yourself, you need help."

Then, just as quickly, she tossed around the idea that maybe she didn't want to get up.

Eventually, Paul and Mary found her once again and came close - staying by her side. They began reminding her of the warm soft sand on Chara, and the cool breezes that refreshed and revived the soul and the skin. They gently lifted her head and whispered stories of life and promises of good times. They quietly listened as Eden told them stories of how miserable and impossible life felt. They didn't judge or negate her words; they stayed with her, held her, and put ointment on the sores the Apalgeo flowers had caused.

Finally, she could lift her head on her own and began to appreciate their help. She drew strength from their reassuring glances and gentle care. Before long, they walked arm in arm back to Chara across the bridge she hadn't seen before.

"That was AWFUL!"

"Yes, Apalgeo is a tricky place that can be very difficult to build a bridge from. It isn't often visited, but did you learn why it might be important?"

Eden was quite at a loss for an answer to this. She tried to explain that all she knew was that if they hadn't been there to help her, she might never have returned to Chara.

"That's right, Apalgeo helps you recognize your need for help."

Eden realized then that the reason she was off Apalgeo at all was because they had joined her and helped her through it. Gratitude welled up within her. So did an awareness that even though she was back on Chara, she was tired. All of today's island hopping had been exhausting. She thanked Paul and Mary for their help and went to bed early.

Discussion Questions

1. Have you ever thought about the reasons that negative emotions might be necessary? Give an example of why feeling each emotion might be necessary (or even good for you).

Anger-

Sadness-

Fear-

Disgust-

Hopeless Despair-

Shame-

2. Describe a time when you felt angry or afraid and then realized you were actually sad underneath it. What did feeling sad do for you? Was it easier to connect with others in sadness than it was in anger or fear? Why do you think so?

3. In the middle of Eden's journey to all the other islands, they return to Chara and rest for a while. Why do you think they rested before visiting the remaining islands? What is the benefit here of rest?

4. Mary explains that in Chara, there is also Eirene. In real life, joy and peace also go hand in hand. Think about a time when you were glad to be with someone and then rested together and felt peace between you. Describe what was happening and try to remember what your body felt like when you experienced joy and peace together with someone.

5. This week, look for times in your day to enjoy quiet together with someone. Pay attention to how it feels and savor it. Start a journal of these quiet moments of peace that you appreciate.

CHAPTER 3

BRIDGE MASTER

While she slept, Eden dreamt. She dreamt about a construction company that specialized in bridge building. When she woke up, she was bewildered by her dream. She was aware that oddly, the bridge builders were mostly women. They were gentle and mild - not at all like the construction workers she was familiar with.

At breakfast, she told the others about her dream but strangely, they didn't seem bewildered by it at all. A hush fell upon the room as an old lady in the corner rolled her wheelchair closer to Eden. Paul got up for a moment and then knelt down in front of the woman. Their eyes met and smiles leapt onto their faces!

Paul said, "Eden, I'd like to introduce you to Yaya. Everything I know, I learned from her."

Yaya was ancient, delicate, and frail. Her piercing blue eyes gazed into Eden's with an intensity greater than anything she had ever felt before. Eden could have sworn she saw the depths of the oceans in Yaya's eyes.

Yaya was everyone's grandmother figure here. No one was certain how old she was, or even who her children had been in her younger days. Every woman learned how to mother from Yaya, and every man learned how to love from her example. She didn't teach like a teacher, but everyone learned from her. She didn't preach like a preacher, but everyone felt closer to God in her embrace. She was the essence of beauty and grace, with a heart bigger than life all contained in one tiny package. The words she spoke, left Eden even more puzzled than she was before.

"I am the bridge master", said Yaya

Then Yaya placed her hands upon Eden's head who felt herself drift into a dreamlike world where time had no meaning.

The bridge master was, above all else, a mother. Eden saw Yaya as a young woman holding her child in her arms, singing softly and gazing into her baby's eyes. This continued for many moons. Yaya's connection with her baby was constant and secure. Soon the baby learned to smile, and it seemed as if they simply practiced smiling at each other for days on end! There was a rhythm to this interaction reminiscent of high and low tides on the shore.

In a flash, she now saw that child as a toddler, walking across bridges with Yaya, back and forth, back and forth, over and over again. The child grew and continued often to cross bridges to each island but never alone. Yaya was right there. Always glad to be with her child. Every time they visited an island together, the bridge became stronger, wider, and it seemed also to be shorter...as if the islands moved closer together with each visit.

Then, Eden noticed that Yaya, the chief bridge master, was not alone with her child on these trips. A man was with them - a father who supported Yaya in her role as bridge master. The father and Yaya loved each other and they loved their child. For them, building bridges was not an afterthought, nor a nuisance, it was their purpose, and one they undertook thoughtfully and intentionally.

In this timeless dreamlike state, Eden watched the child grow up and start to cross her bridges on her own. By now, these were strong and stable and she never seemed to have difficulty returning to Chara.

Eventually this child became a mother herself. The birth of her child promoted her to become the new bridge builder. She shaped her child's bridges based on the ones that Yaya had helped her build for herself.

But as time passed, in her busyness, she stopped visiting one of the islands, and her own bridge grew weak and unstable. The new mother recognized that her own bridge had fallen in disrepair while caring so much for her child's bridges. Rather than hide this weak place, she turned to Yaya for help once again. This weakness became an opportunity for Yaya to show her once more that she was always glad to be with her. Now, with all her bridges repaired and strengthened, she was able to take her own child to that island as well.

Eden awoke with new understanding and more questions bouncing around in her head.

Yaya smiled, "You can ask me anything"

Feeling as if she had known Yaya all along, she comfortably began asking her questions, "So, mothers help build the bridges? But how exactly do you build them?"

"Bridge building is both simple and complex. It's complex because it's so different from anything you've seen before. It's simple because it all stems from Chara."

She paused to let that sink in for a moment before continuing, "You can't build a bridge from the islands themselves. The building always starts on Chara. Being glad to be with someone is stronger than steel. It is more powerful than those large cranes and heavy concrete slabs you may have seen used to make bridges in your world.

The strength we receive on Chara creates in us the capacity we need to be able to make trips to those islands and come back again. All the time you spend on Chara infuses you with a diamond like substance that will be used to create your bridges. Every step on Chara increases your supply. Every step away from Chara disperses that substance into a bridge."

Yaya giggled a bit at what she was about to say.

"If we could make a cartoon to describe things, I think it would look like everyone walking around on straws! We would be drinking in Chara's resources right through our feet and then spitting them out to make our bridges!"

Eden pictured this for a moment and joined Yaya in laughing at this idea.

Yaya continued, "I want you to understand that the more Chara you have, the thicker you can build your bridge. Also, the more times you cross onto your bridge with your Chara refills, the stronger your bridge becomes. Likewise, if your supplies are low, your bridge will be flimsy and fragile. You may even run out of material before you finish constructing the return bridge. This is why it's vital for me to walk on Chara with my child, being glad to be together and gathering supplies for the bridges. Our time together- enjoying one another, playing, laughing, singing, whatever we're doing on Chara, - gives us both the abundant supplies we so desperately need."

Yaya glanced at Eden and saw a childlike curiosity that prompted her to continue.

"As a mother, there are times when my child experiences those things in life that make trips to the other islands necessary; when this happens I have even more reason to be glad to be with her. I cannot fathom abandoning a child when they feel afraid, angry, sad, ashamed, disgusted, or hopeless. Those are times when I know she needs my presence the most. She will need to draw upon my strength and my larger resource of supplies from Chara to get back from the islands. As you can see, my own bridges to those places are quite strong, so I have the capacity and capability to walk with someone who lacks a strong bridge."

With a frown, Yaya added, "But if I had a weak bridge to Lupe, or minimal supplies from Chara, it would be nearly impossible for me to travel back and forth from Lupe carrying my child."

"Wow that seems like a lot of pressure and responsibility on the mother. Don't you ever get tired?"

Yaya leaned back in her chair and looked up at the sky, lost in thought for a while. She then touched Eden's hand and they drifted once again into that dreamlike memory world.

This time Eden saw bridge building trips that the father took. Next, she saw other family members, like grandparents, aunts, and uncles involved in bridge building trips. Yaya's time with the child started the bridge building but after that, others could use what she had already established and build on that. This gave Yaya some time to tend to her own needs and to rest when she was overwhelmed. Bridge building, or rather bridge maintenance, wasn't solely a responsibility of the mother. The entire family got to help!

What stood out the most to Eden was that everyone took on bridge building, bridge maintenance, and bridge repair with a vigor that was uplifting. None of it seemed like a chore to anyone in the family. This attitude was so refreshing, and Eden really liked Chara for this reason. Well, that was one of the reasons anyway. She noticed something else that created yet another question for Yaya.

"I noticed that the children don't build their own bridges, right? Eventually they grow up and the bridge their family built for them becomes their own. How do the bridge builders know what bridge to build and when to build it?"

"Now, that's a great question."

Yaya went on to explain that as the bridge master, she had to understand something called synchronization. "Synchronization is like a magnet between two people. The bridge builder cannot just randomly decide on a trip or say, "Let's go to Orgizo". She must wait for a time when a trip to Orgizo is necessary. The builder can't orchestrate this event; she needs to be able to feel the pull of the island when the time is right. The bridge builder comes alongside the young bridge owner based on the child's needs. Through synchronization, she draws near just like a magnet and carries her supply from Chara with her."

Yaya talked with her hands as she spoke, like a conductor.

"I don't want to confuse you Eden. This synchronization piece is complicated. But it's a crucial component of bridge building. Remember dear, the bridge master is the builder of the new bridge. The young bridge owner brings supplies from Chara, as much as they can gather, but often it is not quite enough. That's why bridge masters have to bring their more abundant supplies. The bridge master has her own bridge, but she wants to help her child build one too. As a mother, she is not just there to get by on hers. She is there to notice and help when she sees her child needs a bridge. When the young bridge owner has a reason to cross onto an island, this synchronization process is what draws the bridge master to her side, like a magnet! Since she has now joined the child on the island, she can use her own supplies to build the bridge back to Chara. This works most easily in the early mothering phase of childhood, but it's possible at any age."

Eden noticed Yaya's hands finally find a resting place in her lap. Yaya sighed a long, slow sigh and said, "I hope that you're starting to see that bridges aren't built in one trip. Building good bridges takes lots of repetition- multiple and frequent trips back and forth. We can't just go somewhere once and check it off our "to do" list. Every trip makes the bridge stronger and more stable."

Yaya's face crinkled as she allowed a frown to etch more creases on her forehead. "We can't stay only on Chara forever. Life requires us to travel to each island quite frequently. Pretending that we don't need to go to an island leaves us with weak bridges back to Chara."

With a pat on Eden's hand, she finished, "You'll learn about weak bridges soon enough."

Eden looked thoughtfully across the ocean at the other islands. "Yaya, this sounds like it works really well in a mother-child situation. But what about someone like me? I don't have any bridges; do I have to go through all this back and forth stuff just like a child?"

As she spoke, the island of Lupe drew closer and she found herself in the foggy place Paul had taken her to just the day before.

Yaya appeared by her side without delay. Her eyes glistened with tears of her own that were on the brink of falling. "It is always sad to think about the places in your own upbringing that led you away from Chara." As she gently rubbed Eden's back, Yaya continued, "I know Dear. It's okay to be sad. I understand how painful it is to think that you have to start right at the beginning."

Yaya's companionship was comforting and as she continued to talk, the two of them began their journey back to Chara. This time, a bridge was being built right beneath Eden's feet.

It was beautiful, really. Her bridge was being built and embossed with the tears that escaped and fell from her eyes; beautiful, gemlike tears of blue...her bridge soon sparkled like the sky above and the waters below.

"It really is amazing how good it feels to have someone who is glad to be with me even when I leave Chara. Just knowing that you were there made it not hurt so much."

"It's my pleasure Eden, it's my pleasure." Yaya took her hand and turned her around to look more closely at her new bridge.

"Look how beautiful your new bridge is. It might be a lot of work to go back and forth, but think of it like a work of art. Our bridges are something to be proud of. As long as you have a bridge builder like me in your life, you will soon have strong bridges from each of the islands. Your work of going back and forth isn't a burden; it's a journey that you can approach with an open heart. Traveling to the other islands is not only necessary, it's one of the most important things you can do. Without visiting each island and building bridges, Chara simply cannot remain Chara. Chara without bridges is nothing more than a fantasy."

With a wink, Yaya excitedly whispered, "Before you know it, you'll be helping others build their bridges and allowing Chara to continue for future generations."

Discussion Questions

1. What kinds of feelings or thoughts arise in you when you hear that mothers are the bridge masters?

2. What kinds of bridges did your mother help you build? What kinds of bridges do you think she had to begin with? Does thinking about your mother's bridge status soften your feelings about your own bridges?

3. After learning where the bridge master gets her supplies...What do you think is the highest priority in bridge building?

4. What do you think would happen if you made being glad to be together a priority in your relationships?

5. Why can't we just try not to feel negative emotions (never build bridges)?

6. Describe a time when you felt someone synchronize with you or you synchronized with someone else.

7. While doing something you enjoy, tell someone that you are glad to be with them this week. Make eye contact as you say it and pay attention both to how they respond and to how that response makes you feel.

10. Are you willing to do the "back and forth" work that is necessary to build bridges? Write out a letter or prayer asking someone you know to help you build your bridges. You might discover that you need to ask different people for help with different bridges. That's okay too. You can keep this letter private if you want to.

CHAPTER 4

BROKEN BRIDGES

Let's use your new bridge to Lupe as an example of a bridge that's still weak. We've made only one trip on this bridge; right? Even though it is beautiful and it was enough to get you back to Chara this time, it's still a brand new bridge. See how it sways in the wind? It strains every section as far as it can be stretched without breaking. This bridge was perfect for the short, small trip you just took to Lupe. But look what happens to it in a storm."

Suddenly a strong gust of wind blew and tossed the bridge about like a flag. Pieces became tattered and tore off, flying out of sight within minutes.

"Oh no!" Eden cried, "This is awful! It hardly took any wind at all for my bridge to fall apart like wet paper."

"That's what happens when bridges haven't been used enough, They don't have the strength to handle any extra pressure. Weak bridges don't have the capacity to get you safely back to Chara in the midst of a storm."

Eden looked as if she needed more explanation, so Yaya continued.

"The capacity and strength of one's bridges is in direct proportion with the amount of supplies brought from Chara. Without adequate supplies from Chara, there is no such thing as strong bridges. One block from Chara gives you one bridge layer...which can handle one "stormy travel day" or a size one storm so to speak."

"Okay," Eden prompted...

"Ten blocks from Chara give you ten bridge layers, which can handle ten stormy travel days OR one size ten storm!" finished Yaya.

Eden thought about the large, strong bridges that could withstand hurricanes and even earthquakes. She imagined that if she had bridges like that, all the awful reasons in the world to leave Chara wouldn't matter, nothing would break her bridges or keep her away from Chara any longer than necessary. Having a strong bridge would mean she would return quickly and safely. She looked at her own tiny bridge and fully understood why her bridge just didn't have the capacity to withstand more than a breeze before collapsing. Eden was now utterly convinced that taking all those back and forth trips was absolutely necessary in order to build a stronger bridge. She was also surer than ever that she wanted more time to live on Chara.

Yaya however, still had a furrowed brow, and Eden knew that there was still more to it than that.

"Come Dear, let's sit for a while, I have more to teach you."

Eden sat beside Yaya on a bench at the Marina. She closed her eyes and at Yaya's touch her head began to swoon again. What she saw next caused her heart to sink, but she remained in the safety of Yaya's reach and let the images unfold in her imagination anyway.

As she took in the scene, she once again saw bridge builders, but instead of loving, honest bridge builders, she saw imposters.

They were people who said they could help to build bridges, but in reality, these imposters didn't bring materials from Chara. Their bridge supplies were nothing but flimsy fabrications from an unnamed island. The imposters fooled the bridge owners, who believed that their supplies would make their bridges strong. They didn't realize that these imposters weren't actually glad to be with them; they were oblivious to the pretense and didn't discover the deception in time.

Eventually storms came and their bridges were entirely washed away leaving them stranded and cut off from Chara.

Now Eden knew exactly why Yaya had frowned when she sat down to teach her.

There were entire communities that hardly ever came back to Chara. They had no way to get there.

A chilling thought floated to the front of Eden's mind. "Was she one of those people?" Eden peeked at Yaya to see if she knew more than she was telling, but Yaya's eyes remained closed.

Yaya said, "There is something just as bad as being stranded on the other islands. Look here at the people who float just offshore." Eden followed Yaya's gaze. "They can't seem to stay on Chara for more than a minute or two. They aren't here long enough to get bridge supplies, nor do they have any bridge builders that they can reach out to. They struggle daily, paddling their boats from island to island, aching for the chance to rest on land. Not only are they stranded, but they are also in danger of being tossed about in the stormy waters. There is no Eirene for those who linger at the edge of Chara in their lifeboats.

"Can't we just go and grab them and bring them here? They are so close, it seems like it would be simple to help them?"

Sighing deeply, Yaya answered, "It does appear as if that would be an obvious solution doesn't it? But it's not that easy. They won't look at us. They keep their eyes firmly on their boat and don't connect or receive from those that do reach out to pull them onto Chara. Chara's magic works best through the eyes."

Eden thought back to how much everyone on Chara had already influenced her. She had believed the power was in their smiles, but now that she thought about it again, she realized it was in their eyes. That was it; the secret to Chara was in the eyes! Every connection started with eye contact.

Yaya looked at Eden and now she felt the connection instantly. She nodded, wordlessly, and let Yaya know that she was finally starting to get it.

"Okay, so we've got imposters building faulty bridges and people more focused on their escape plans than on each other. Is that it? Does everyone else have a nice strong bridge system in place?"

Yaya looked grave, "I'm afraid not. In fact, the primary reason for weak bridges is inadequate bridge maintenance. As people grow older, they sometimes take their bridges for granted and stop going back and forth across them. They begin to devalue the importance of going to certain islands and refuse to go when the time comes. Other times, they stop returning to Chara, and when this happens, their return bridge falls into disrepair. The normal sea level changes during high tide and low tide will take down some of these less used bridges and at first, no one will even notice. It doesn't require a large storm to destroy a bridge that isn't being maintained. We see this happen a lot during the teen years. Adolescence is well known for a lack of bridge maintenance."

"So, what does good bridge maintenance look like?"

"Not going alone." answered Yaya.

"Sometimes you go with a more experienced bridge builder, at other times you're with a newer bridge builder. But no matter what, true bridge maintenance never gives into the thought "I don't need anyone else to handle this."

"But wait! What about the times when there really isn't anyone around to go with you? What if you are alone when it's time to go to one of the other islands?"

"Oh dear, I promise I'll get to that soon enough! Don't you worry Eden...there is more to the secrets of Chara than I have yet revealed! First, you need to understand what happens when you're away from Chara for too long."

Yaya tried to explain, "Sometimes telling people about life away from Chara doesn't go over so well. If they are on Chara, they don't want to leave and can't understand what it would be like to stay away. But if they are already away then they don't usually want to hear an explanation of what is happening to them. I'm afraid that in order for you to understand this, you're going to have to experience it for yourself. This will be difficult Eden, but I want you to know that I'm right here and I'm not going to let you stay away forever. I'm going to let you taste it in a dream and when you wake up, I'll share the most precious secret Chara still holds."

Eden agreed to let Yaya give her a dream, and they parted ways for the evening.

That night Eden enjoyed some time alone in her room, listening to music and painting. She had always longed to be an artist but had never taken the time to try to paint before now. As she explored the different textures and colors of the paints, she found that she felt alive. She laughed at her mistakes and stood back to admire the places where she was able to turn her mistakes into something beautiful.

As the evening grew darker, Eden started to get tired. She knew her dreams might be a little scary tonight so she decided to turn in early. To her surprise, she wasn't afraid of the night ahead of her. She still had that peaceful Eirene feeling inside and drifted off to sleep easily.

The smell of smoke filled her nostrils even before she opened her eyes and a frown had etched lines into her forehead. Her shoulders were tense, and her stomach in knots. Waking like this was utterly absurd! Groaning and muttering curses under her breath, Eden awoke on Orgizo. She felt entirely justified in her anger and in the grumpiness that overtook her.

"How dare they kick her off that nice beach?"

She was driven solely by the desire to yell at someone but realized she was alone. Standing on the shore of Orgizo, she looked towards Chara with total disdain. Since she had no bridge on which to travel back, she picked up some rocks in frustration and hurled them towards the sea with a scream.

"Doesn't anyone notice that I'm gone? I can't believe they would let this happen."

In annoyance, she moaned at how hot she was getting. Not even the water at the shoreline could offer relief. Instead of being cooling, it was hot - almost boiling. Her attempts to cool herself were starting to look futile.

"Perhaps I can find shade further inland," she thought to herself.

To her dismay, she discovered that as she journeyed inland the temperatures became even hotter and fires burst forth from within the earth itself.

"Great, I'm stuck here with no way of escaping this ridiculous heat!" she thought, and flopped herself down to sit on the ashy beach, very miserable.

Days and nights passed, and still alone and angry she sat.

One day she got up, brushed the ashes from her lower half, and started walking along the shore.

"I need to make a shelter or something. I might as well make a home for myself here."

As she walked to the opposite side of Orgizo, she found some palm fronds that were still unscathed and she took them to make a shelter. It wasn't much, but at least it blocked the sun's rays. She settled in and did her best to get comfortable. Time no longer seemed to matter. Every minute of every day away from Chara, Eden was losing who she was and starting more and more to resemble Orgizo. Her face became crinkled and dry, her eyes squinted and harsh. It was a good thing there weren't any mirrors, or Eden surely would have broken them all by now. Life on Orgizo was hardly becoming cozy, but Chara was now just a distant place that she no longer even desired to get back to.

Orgizo had now become her home. She barely noticed the pungent smell of the fires and smoke anymore. She had grown accustomed to the heat and was becoming comfortable with how things were. She discovered others on Orgizo, too. They were loud and obnoxious at first, but the more she pretended to like them, the more they seemed to like her too.

In fact, a lot of pretending was going on and pretending eventually became her new normal. Everyone walked around with big smiles and made jokes. She heard echoes of what she had experienced on Chara, but when you really looked into people's eyes, you glimpsed a brief flicker of their pain before they quickly turned away. That inviting spark was completely missing.

Of course, tempers ran high and there were daily fights on Orgizo. It was a widely held belief that each person possessed the right to explode over everyone else when things didn't go their way.

Indifferent to the feelings of others, no-one cared if their "temper spill" affected those around them. In the middle of all the pretending, fake smiles and explosions, everyone was in pain.

Eden soon learned that many methods had been devised for dealing with this pain. Some found a bit of relief in the sweet of the cocoa tree; others discovered the excitement and playfulness that alcohol or drugs brought. Some people turned to the rules of religion or chasing success in the hope of finding relief. Still others found that sex and relationships could give them a form of pleasure and spent all their time seeking another one of these kinds of experiences. They had a fun name for all these ways to numb their pain- BEEPS, and to all outward appearances, they used their BEEPS proudly and without shame.

Eden began numbing her pain with a bit of what she called harmless partying. The excitement of nightlife helped her erase the memory of what she was losing with each day spent away from Chara. Every night she found a rush in a new drink, a new pill, or a new man. But every night seemed to start earlier than the last until eventually she needed to party as soon as she woke up to avoid feeling miserable. Sadly, it seemed that her party life and all her BEEPS weren't actually enough to remove the pain of life away from Chara.

Eden felt even more miserable than she did before she felt compelled to start looking for BEEPS.

The strange thing was that even though Chara and the other inhabitants of Orgizo were just across the bay from Chara, everyone she met found ways to get to all the islands apart from Chara. It was almost as if Chara had disappeared from their radar. These people had boats that went from Orgizo to Phobos and Apalgeo all the time, but no one looked twice at Chara anymore.

Only at night, under the cover of darkness, did Eden allow herself briefly to remember the "good old days". It was then that she would briefly shed a tear before seeking more relief from the pain with her BEEPS.

Discussion Questions

1. In this chapter, Yaya describes a direct proportion between time spent on Chara and the capacity and strength of one's bridge. Think about your own experience with joy. If I tell you that joyful experiences, where someone is glad to be with you, get put in a bucket called "joy strength" and that bucket grows to contain more and more without spilling or cracking, what size bucket would you think that you have? It can range in size from water bottle lid to a swimming pool and greater!

2. Do you see a link between your "joy strength" and your ability to recover from negative emotions? On a sheet of paper, draw a map of your own Joy and Neighboring Islands. Then draw your bridges to each emotion. Some bridges may be stronger than others. Draw two bridges for each island- one going AWAY from Joy and one going TOWARDS Joy. They can (and probably will) be different sizes. Drawing this map can help you to see which bridges you need help with and which bridges you might be able to help others build. There is a sample map in Appendix B as an example. If you're an artist, go all out with this exercise! Paint, mixed media, clay- whatever helps you see it best!

3. How much eye contact do you receive on a daily basis? Keep a record of it for one week. There is a tracking journal in Appendix C to help you. You will also be tracking how your "joy strength" felt on those days. Did you find a link?

4. Can you relate to Eden's decision to go ahead and "get comfortable" while she was stranded away from Chara? Why do you think she (or you) decided to do that instead of seeking a way back?

5. BEEPS is an acronym that my father Ed Khouri coined. It stands for the Behaviors, Events, Experiences, People and Substances that people use to get some "fake joy" for their brain. Have you ever used BEEPS to help you ease your pain or lack of joy? How long did it "help" you feel better? Did it ever make you more miserable?

6. Understanding why we do the things we do can help us become tender toward ourselves, instead of just pretending that it's not happening. Is it understandable for Eden to do things like "seek shelter", "seek companionship", and "seek relief from her pain"? If you're up to it, consider writing yourself a letter of "understanding" in the space below about any decisions you've made in your situations that didn't lead you back to joy.

CHAPTER 5

RETURNING

Meanwhile, back on Chara, Yaya watched Eden toss and turn in her sleep. She reached down and gently caressed her hand as if to offer comfort and support even while she slept. This dream lesson was a hard one, and Yaya couldn't help but think of the many people she'd lost to the suffering of being away from Chara, the suffering Eden was now experiencing in her dream. As the bridge master it was heart-breaking to see so many choose to stick with a deceptive sense of "comfortable" rather than returning to or discovering Chara.

But for Eden, this was just a lesson, a dream, and it was now time for things to turn around.

Sleeping on Orgizo was always a problem. Falling asleep, staying asleep, and then waking up all posed their own separate issues. This day was no different. Eden became more aware than usual of just how exhausted she was. She stretched her arms up to the sun and felt a jolt of pain run through her back and neck.

With an overly loud cry of frustration, she groaned to no one in particular, "I'm so sick of being here".

Suddenly an answering thought popped into her head, "Then let's go back to Chara".

The thought of Chara brought tears to her eyes and she found herself on Lupe almost instantly. Instead of fighting it, this time she gave in. She sat down, wrapped her arms around herself, and let the tears fall.

She really missed the people she had met on Chara. Deep inside she could feel an empty spot in her heart as she thought about them. The damp air here on Lupe felt quite soothing on her skin and the view across the foggy bay was actually quite beautiful. Eden leaned back against the sand, closed her eyes, and breathed in deeply. Her tears came steadily, but finally releasing them began to calm and relax her.

With her eyes closed, and her breathing slowed, she began to sense for the first time that she wasn't really alone. There was a softening taking place in her heart, and it was spreading into her thoughts as well. She felt comforted- simply by the air she was breathing in.

All at once, she felt someone take her hand. She kept her eyes shut, it was comforting to feel the presence of someone else, and she didn't want to ruin the moment by checking to see if it was truly a person or all in her imagination.

Suddenly she heard Yaya speaking softly in her sweet old lady voice, "I've missed you too".

Eden opened her eyes and hungrily threw her arms around Yaya in an embrace that felt sure to save her life. She sobbed harder than she had before and fully felt the anguish of all that she had lost whilst away from Chara. Yaya WAS there and she understood it all, all that Eden had been through.

"Oh, how wonderful it feels to be understood!"

Without words being exchanged, Eden knew deep in the recesses of her mind that this woman GOT her. There was something within her, something in her gaze and in the way she embraced her, that soothed and nourished the aches and pains within her soul. She didn't have to say a word.

"Come child," whispered Yaya, "Come back to Chara with me today".

Hand in hand, they crossed Yaya's strong and established bridge.

"You're gonna need to get some supplies from Chara so you can build you some bridges!"

Just then Eden awoke in her bed and looked up to see Yaya smiling at her.

"Oh Yaya" Eden exclaimed, "I had forgotten it was all a dream! It felt so very real".

"Yes dear one, I know." She placed a robe on the edge of the bed and continued, "Once you've had some breakfast we shall talk about all you experienced and the things you learned."

The smell of pancakes reached Eden's nose and her stomach rumbled in response. She got out of bed, slipped into the robe and walked out onto the back porch to join Yaya for breakfast.

They ate in silence as Eden mulled over her dream. It was certainly unlike any other dream she'd ever had. It was not fading at all. Eden considered how easy it had been to walk away from Chara and not even look for a way back. The intensity of her feelings had over-ruled all logic to the point where all she could see were things that justified her anger. It had even reached the point where she honestly believed she wanted nothing more to do with Chara.

"Yaya, something is really baffling me. After I was tired of being angry, and ended up crying, I got to a point where I felt like I wasn't alone anymore. But this was before you arrived, and I don't understand that".

Yaya smiled gently and her eyes met Eden's. "You weren't alone. In fact, we are never truly alone. What you began to experience was an awareness – an awareness of the sweetest gift in this land. You felt our beloved Pneuma. Pneuma is our friend, our helper, our link to all that is Chara and Eirene."

Puzzled, Eden tilted her head with an inquisitive look that prompted Yaya to elaborate.

"Pneuma is the one I mentioned to you before – Chara's most treasured secret. He can help us build bridges even if no-one else is around at the time. In fact, Pneuma is the true master when it comes to bridge building. He is the magic that takes your tears and inlays them in such a beautiful way onto the bridges. He is the foundation and source of joy!"

She continued, "Above all, Pneuma loves to comfort us and bring us together with others. It was Pneuma that brought me into your dream to be with you and bring you home."

"Then why didn't he come to get me from Orgizo? Why didn't he just bring me back to Chara right away?"

Before Yaya could answer, a knock at the door interrupted their discussion. Paul and Mary had come to see Eden and find out how she was doing.

Paul's eyes creased up as he smiled at Eden with fatherly eyes. Eden jumped up from her seat and found herself lifted off the ground in his strong bear hug. Mary was carrying a bouquet of wildflowers she must have picked on their way over. She went straight to the kitchen and put them in water.

"Eden, I hope you like these flowers!" she shouted over the sound of running water. "I thought of you when I saw them and I just had to bring them by".

Eden felt a surge of joy as she interacted with them both. They knew all about what she and Yaya had been doing for the past twenty-four hours, but they didn't come to press her for details. They came to simply be with her and enjoy her company.

"I love them!" she answered, "Thank-you so much. In fact, look at this painting I was playing around with last night". Everyone followed Eden into the living room to see her painting of flowers, just like the ones Mary held in her hand.

For the next half an hour or so, they sat around, enjoying and appreciating each other's company and sharing stories of other times that they had each appreciated. This spontaneous conversation left Eden feeling more refreshed than the pancake breakfast.

As they told tales of times when they had received gifts, or watched sunsets, or laughed together over something silly, Eden felt joy and peace continuing to steadily grow inside her.

"That story reminds me of a time when...." was heard time after time around the room. These stories of appreciation were truly contagious.

Mary then shared a story with a slightly different tone.

"I remember this one time when I walked into the bathroom to find my daughter, who was around 3 years old at the time, covered in lipstick. Not only was she covered, but the wall was covered as well! Oh my, was I upset! I found myself very quickly on Orgizo, fuming at the mess I was surely going to have to spend hours cleaning up. I couldn't believe how angry it made me."

Eden instantly thought of her recent dream about living on Orgizo and wondered where this story was going to end up.

"Then I remembered just how much she loved to draw and how her eyes would light up when we did art together, looking for my approval as she colored or painted. My anger subsided rapidly as I walked back across my bridge to deal with the mess she had made. I was so glad to remember her innocence and delight in that moment. Instead of losing myself to Orgizo, I was able to smile at her, laugh with her and enjoy being with her as we oohed and ahhed over her masterpieces. Of course, we had to clean it up together, but the joy I felt in seeing her pleasure over her "artwork" was more than worth the effort that cleaning up took".

Yaya's laughter filled the room during Mary's story. She had so many similar experiences that came flooding back as she listened.

"Oh how I love a good "return to Chara" story!"

Then she went on to explain just what had made this story different from all the others.

"Eden honey, did you notice that this story didn't take place only on Chara? Did you see how Mary actually ended up appreciating something that at first made her mad?"

"Yes, I noticed that right away. How exactly did she do that? In my dream when I went to Orgizo on my own I could only see the things that made me mad."

Eager to help Eden gain understanding Mary said, "There is power in appreciation! When we take small trips to the other islands, we can use our appreciation memories to help us cross our bridge back to Chara. When we were all talking and sharing stories, did you become aware that you too began to feel some of the same feelings we were talking about?"

"Yes, it was like each story sparked a similar experience in my memories and turned it on".

"Exactly", interjected Paul. "We practice appreciation for that very purpose. When we appreciate one thing, it sometimes triggers memories of other things we appreciate. The more often we do this here on Chara, the more natural it is to do this even when we leave Chara."

THANKFULNESS & GRATITUDE
APPRECIATION

At once, Eden remembered the moment in her dream when she felt appreciation for the coolness and the beauty of the fog on Lupe. Although it hadn't occurred to her at the time, she realized now that this was when things began to change. Somewhere within her, that feeling of appreciation had begun to soothe and quiet all the other negative feelings. It was very subtle, barely noticeable at the time, but it did happen. Recalling it now made the experience feel even more pronounced than it had felt originally.

Yaya said, "Appreciation is one of the most basic tools you can use to maintain your bridge, especially on the smaller, less overwhelming trips to the islands."

"Oh wow" Eden exclaimed, "It just clicked in my head- since we use what we pick up on Chara to build our bridges- OF COURSE remembering the things we appreciate would also help build our bridges!" Without taking a breath as she was unpacking this revelation, Eden continued, "I remember you saying that time spent on Chara gave us "blocks" to build our bridge with…. Sooooooo, are you now saying that we can have one block for each moment and then when we remember it, it's like we get a whole 'nother block from the memory?"

"Yes!" all three of them exclaimed!

"That's exactly right. Our joyful moments give us what we need, and then remembering them RESUPPLIES us all over again!" Yaya beamed with pride at Eden for coming to this realization on her own.

She grabbed Eden's hand in her own and assured her, "Remembering often the things you appreciate makes it easier to recall them when you have journeyed to the other islands. You haven't had much practice with this, so it makes total sense that your experience in your dream left you stranded."

Mary added, "In the story I shared with you about my daughter's lipstick extravaganza, I could remember that I loved her even when I was upset with her because I have been doing this all my life. Learning how to keep hold of that didn't happen overnight. Over time, and after many bridge building trips, I learned that these trips to the other islands are just temporary and much of what feels so important when you are on those islands is not nearly as important as what I experience on Chara. This knowledge is now so deeply rooted that it enables me to be able to draw from memories of appreciation because I know that who I am is more powerful than how irritated I may feel at the time. Who I am is her mother, and loving her is part of who I am, that doesn't change just because I'm angry."

Eden really wanted to learn how to do this. For some reason it sounded so much easier for them.

Yaya, who always seemed to be able read her mind, rolled her chair over to the window and said, "We want you to be able to do this too, but it will take time. Even as you listen to our stories and descriptions of life on Chara there is still a part of you that believes that you don't have whatever it is that makes our world work. There is a part of you that feels as if we're better than you are, or that you aren't good enough to actually build bridges and maintain them no matter how nice it sounds. But Eden, you're wrong. You're very wrong. Look at me, look at Paul, and Mary... we are here for you and we can see things in you that you can't yet see or feel. This doesn't make us better than you; it only means that we are more experienced than you are. This gives us the honor of being able to encourage you to keep looking up because we remember what it was like to be in your shoes once before."

Eden didn't know how to respond or how to take anything in, she felt kind of frozen inside and expected to end up on another island but couldn't figure out which one to land on, Phobos or Entrope, or maybe even Lupe, they all seemed applicable. Much of what Yaya had said did feel true and that realization was strangely freeing. Eden didn't sense any judgment from her, only compassion.

Yaya took her silence for permission to continue.

"Remember when I told you about our Pneuma?"

Eden nodded, she did remember. Just hearing his name caused her to feel complete and whole in spite of her inadequacies.

Discussion Questions

1. How did allowing herself to leave Orgizo in order to go to Lupe impact Eden? Do you think feeling sad about a situation might be beneficial?

2. When have you experienced a negative emotion and had someone really understand your feelings? Did you notice any change in your outlook when someone connected with you in your pain? If you can remember, write down a short description of how it felt when you knew they "got it".

3. In this chapter, Yaya, Paul and Mary shared "appreciation stories" with Eden. This is your chance to write one for yourself. Share it with someone in your family or your group this week. An appreciation story has four parts. A description of what was happening, how it made you feel- use lots of adjectives, how your body felt when you experienced those feelings, and then what you did in response. . The more detail you can give, the more your body will respond in the same manner, restoring that state of appreciation to your system.

> *For example: I was in the mountains hiking with a friend. We had just gotten to a resting place with a great view. I felt content, relaxed, and genuinely happy. My body felt light, calm, I smiled, and my breathing rate slowed down. In response, I remember thanking her for being with me and laying down on a large rock to enjoy the moment*

4. Use Appendix D to keep track of what causes you to feel appreciation five times this week.

5. In the story Paul says, "When we appreciate one thing, sometimes it triggers us into remembering something else we appreciate". Do you think this is only true of positive memories or do you think that when we share and think about negative memories, more negative memories and feelings will be triggered? How can being aware of this help?

6. Have you ever "seen" something in someone you loved that they couldn't see for themselves?

7. Are you more like Mary or Eden when it comes to being able to "return to joy"? If you are like Mary, write an example of a Return to Joy Story (just like an appreciation story, but includes a short mention of what upset you at first followed by how you "returned" to joy.) If you are more like Eden, and have more experience with being stuck in negative emotions, just spend five minutes remembering an appreciation story. (You can use the one in question three, or just recall another one without writing it down).

CHAPTER 6

WITH US

"My favorite thing about Pneuma is knowing that He is always glad to be with us. He is the wisest, most patient and loving teacher you'll ever have. He's the best friend you'll ever meet and He's always an advocate for who you really are. He is the glue that holds Chara together as a community."

Yaya had moved and was sitting directly in front of Eden and a hush had fallen on the room. Eden didn't move a muscle as she listened intently to Yaya's description of Pneuma. Whenever Yaya spoke of him, she felt drawn like a magnet to know more.

"Pneuma is especially interested in helping people that haven't yet built bridges back to Chara. Earlier today before Paul and Mary arrived, you asked me a profound question. Do you remember it?"

"Yes," Eden replied, "I wanted to know why Pneuma didn't just bring me back to Chara himself, and why he waited until I was on Lupe to come and help me. It seemed like such a waste to make me suffer so long. I mean, honestly, why not just help me right away?"

The anger and disdain that she heard in her own voice for what he hadn't done took her by surprise. Only seconds before, she was feeling in awe of him, and now here she was upset with Him. This was so confusing!

"I can hear your anguish tinged with anger as you remember suffering on Orgizo alone," said Yaya.

"I think talking about it stirs up my "right to be angry" feelings, just as I felt on Orgizo when I realized I had been left there alone."

Panic rose within her and she groaned, "Perhaps this question is going to take me away from Chara again." All of her was now becoming tense, her shoulders, her stomach and she could feel the creases in her forehead deepen more than usual.

Paul and Mary, who were sitting on either side of Eden, each took one of her hands in theirs and reassured her.

"You are safe here, where we are glad to be with you."

They explained that joy was present in the room and that none of the emotions she cycled through were going to take her away from Chara. They were glad to be with her as she was learning and this connection between them all was strong enough to keep her on Chara.

"There is strength in numbers little one." whispered Mary.

Yaya urged Eden to trust her. "Look at me Eden; look at my face and into my eyes. Do you see that you are not alone?"

Eden complied and nodded while stifling some tears.

"I do understand what you're feeling. I understand because I can see and feel your pain. It is because of Pneuma that I can do this. He is the one who created these bridges and islands and He knows everything that takes place on them. He was there with you on Orgizo, you just didn't know it."

Eden was frustrated and still didn't understand, "Why didn't he just MAKE me know it?"

Paul replied, "He doesn't make us do anything. He gives us the freedom to choose between the messages our emotions are sending to us, and who we really are. The existence of the other islands never changes our real nature, even though when we are stuck away from Chara for too long, we start to believe that we *are* where we live. Pneuma wants us to live on Chara with Him, and with each other, he knows that who we are is developed most completely on Chara, but He doesn't want it to be a prison."

Eden sighed and looked down at her feet, "I guess I don't want it to be a prison either."

He continued, "Everything that you like about Chara, comes from Him. Do you remember how you liked the way that we all related to one another – the way our faces lit up when we saw each other and how we laughed together and supported one another? These joyful interactions stem from our friendship with Pneuma. This is how He treats us. When He looks at us and is glad to be with us, we become more like Him. His nature kindles the desire in us to extend His joy to one another. Just as he sparked the desire in your heart when you saw it for the first time."

Eden did remember all of that, and as she thought about it, she became aware that there was in fact, a spark inside of her. This spark felt like a good thing, not at all like the painful burning on Orgizo. It was a pleasing sensation, warm and inviting, and she wanted more of it.

She closed her eyes and began to recall her experience of Pneuma on Lupe. She remembered how comforting it felt when she realized she wasn't alone. A calming took place in her mind. The confusion that had been surging and raging internally quieted in that moment.

The others quietly watched her sitting there on the couch with her eyes closed. They saw the muscles in her face soften, her shoulders relax, and her breathing rate slow down.

"Are you aware of His presence now?" Yaya whispered

The smile on Eden's face was their clear answer. They just let her stay in this quiet place.

Eden felt more settled now. She was conscious of her breath - Pneuma's breath. Her breath seemed different now that she was with Him. It was fuller, deeper and felt more in tune with her natural state. Breathing in with Pneuma was restorative, and reset her back to the start before she ever had ever known pain or disappointment, or lies.

Time seemed to stand still as the connection with Pneuma deepened until Eden connected fully with him for the first time. What she had experienced on Lupe was like a hint of His essence carried on the wind. Now, as she breathed with Him she felt it was almost like being in the womb again. She felt weightless - suspended in the warmth of His love.

A voice unlike any she had heard before echoed in her thoughts, "Welcome, little one". As she began to know Him, she sensed a tenderness in His voice that felt melodic. She realized that knowing Him didn't come from long drawn out interviews and questions. Knowing Him was found through the connection she was experiencing with Him. She didn't have to ask questions, she just knew.

Pneuma showed her his face; it was unlike any she had known before. Light emanated from His eyes and poured into her heart filling it with a joy she never knew existed. His face was not "solid" like the human, physical sense and it was hard to distinguish any features other than His smile and His eyes. More than handsome, He was breathtaking- no, not breathtaking, BREATH-GIVING!

She opened her eyes to see if those around her were still in fact there. It felt as if hours had gone by. The smiles of Yaya, Paul, and Mary met her glance. Without a word being spoken, they knew that she was meeting Pneuma and their expressions danced in merriment for her and encouraged her to continue.

Pneuma again whispered deeply into her soul, "You are always welcome here. I have prepared this place for you and me to meet whenever you want to. In fact, I am with you always and I carry this place with me wherever we go. This meeting place is where I can breathe life into you and repair the places where you feel broken. It is here that you will begin to know me, and you will discover who you are. Would you like that?"

Unsure if she needed to answer aloud or not, Eden simply nodded.

"My voice is inside you, and your voice is also there. You can speak to me in silence, or shout declarations for all to hear. Whatever you feel comfortable with, what is natural to you, is what I want for you. I will never ask you to be different than who you are".

Eden was amazed at the way Pneuma knew her thoughts before she had even had time to think them fully herself. It was a relief that He knew her so well. She no longer needed to untangle her own inner struggles of "what to say", and it gave her a sense of freedom she'd never considered possible before.

She leaned into Him, resting against His chest as He began to show her things that answered her questions. It wasn't so much that He answered her questions; it was more like her questions were no longer necessary because she knew His love.

He knew that eventually she would have questions again, and that was okay. He was especially good at reminding people of moments past when they wanted Him more than they wanted answers.

It occurred to Eden that questions were in some ways strange things - often driving us hard to possess information that would not truly benefit us. With Pneuma, questions that were beneficial to us were answered, and questions that would lead us down dangerous roads were washed away. The best part however, was that no matter what and at all times, He was glad to be with her, and she with him.

He would gaze upon her with the same deep attention a small child would give a butterfly. Pneuma was her biggest fan. Even when she stumbled, His warm smile would be enough to soothe her hurts and quiet her fears.

As they sat there together, memories of her life flashed before her. Occasions when she had felt alone and when she had been hurt. Pneuma was the one who led her to those memories and gently showed her His heart and intention during those moments. Most of all, He showered her with His love, and comforted her gently.

When the question of "Why didn't you just show yourself then" arose once more, Eden saw an impression of herself as a younger child with a deep scrape on her knee. Dirt and gravel were deeply embedded into the wound. Though the pain was great, the thought of someone touching her damaged tissue and taking out the pieces of gravel was even more terrifying and overwhelming. Then she saw Pneuma, like a loving Father, kneeling next to her wounded knee. He was there with her patiently letting her know what to expect, explaining that He would be gentle and that He wasn't going to do anything she didn't say yes to. He promised her that He would just remain there, and would wait for her permission to begin the process.

She appreciated His gentleness; His reassurance, the way He loved her and inspired her to trust Him. It took some time, but eventually she built up her strength and courage and finally said "Yes" and allowed Him to help her. He blew gently on the wound, and locked eyes with her the entire time. Slowly and with the soft and sure touch of a skilled surgeon, he removed the debris and cleaned her wound before breathing healing and new life into her skin once more.

No longer did that accusatory question bubble up within her. She trusted Him, His timing, and most of all His love.

Even though only an hour or two had passed since she first recalled discovering His presence with her on Lupe, all of these lessons and realizations had now come to the forefront of who she was and begun to shape her identity. She was loved and cherished by the Great Pneuma! He was trustworthy, and gentle and strong. Whatever He said about her was the ultimate truth and it resonated deep inside like a chorus of angels resounding with a deep "Yes". The truth He spoke was that she was a delight to Him! In response, she delighted in Him.

At this first meeting, the impact of "knowing" had less to do with protecting her from the unknown, and everything to do with becoming intimately understood at depths beyond her wildest dreams.

Eden opened her eyes again and became aware of her damp cheeks. She rested her head on Mary's shoulder and knew that she didn't need to explain what had just happened.

Yaya handed her a gift and kissed her on the forehead. "This is for you Eden. While Pneuma is always with you, it will be helpful for you to record some of what you experienced in that place He created for the two of you to meet. As we've explained before, remembering is a beautiful, yet fleeting thing. As a young Charanian, I'd like to encourage you to use this journal to help you remember. Write down what He tells you, and what you discover in His presence."

Eden unwrapped the journal and breathed in the scent of the soft leather cover. "Thank-you. I will cherish this gift Yaya. I don't ever want to forget what I'm feeling right now."

"I want to show you one more thing" Yaya beckoned them all to join her on the beach.

Paul pushed Yaya's wheelchair as they walked together in silence for a while. When they got to the Marina, Yaya pointed to a set of golden bridges Eden hadn't noticed before. They were larger than any of the other bridges she had seen before. They reached high up in the sky, almost touching the clouds.

"Those are Pneuma's bridges".

"Pneuma has bridges too?" this thought had never occurred to Eden.

"Yes, and His bridges are perfectly constructed. They have unlimited capacity and no storm will affect them. His bridges are here for you to use as you need them."

Eden's mouth dropped open in shock. "Really?"

Paul laughed aloud at her response with gladness, "You will love this Eden, don't you worry!" and prompted Yaya to continue.

"Bridge building is Pneuma's specialty even more so than it is mine. It is His delight to be able to help you return to Chara whenever you feel weak on your own bridges. He can travel effortlessly to any of the islands, and you are never alone. Since He is with you, connect with Him and let Him bring you back to Chara." Yaya's voice oozed with encouragement.

Eden felt an excitement blended with a hopefulness that could never be destroyed begin to take root in her soul. Pneuma WAS always with her and always glad to be with her. She realized that Pneuma is the very essence of Chara and that NOTHING could separate her from Chara because she literally carried it inside of her.

Discussion Questions

1. Mary tells Eden that there is "strength in numbers". How does being with others increase our capacity?

2. Can you relate to Eden's anger and confusion over why Pneuma didn't rescue her right away? What did you think about Paul's response to her?

3. What enabled Eden to fully connect with Pneuma?

4. Have you ever experienced a moment with God that helped you KNOW He was there? Write about how you felt. If you haven't yet experienced that, write about a time when you felt peaceful and ask Him where He was at that time. Use this space to also journal any response you feel.

5. Is it possible that experiencing "glad to be with you" from within your spirit connection with God could make becoming stranded without a bridge an impossibility? How hopeful does this make you for the future?

6. Use this page to write down any closing thoughts you have after finishing this book. What stood out to you the most? What impacted you the most? Ask the Holy Spirit to show you HIS bridges and then ask for permission to use them when you need them.

7. Journaling is a gift for anyone. Treat yourself to purchasing a beautiful journal that you can begin recording your own experiences with Pneuma.

Appendix A: Glossary

Anoia (I u ne ya)- The Greek word for the emotion of disgust. Also used as an island name. Disgust is one of the Big Six negative emotions that we experience.

Apalgeo (Ap el jay o)- Greek word for being "past feeling, ceasing to care" which is a lot like the emotion of hopeless despair. Also used as an island name. Hopeless despair is one of the Big Six negative emotions that we experience.

BEEPS- This is the term Ed Khouri uses to describe the attachments to Behaviors, Events, Experiences, People, or Substances that we use to regulate our emotions, increase our pleasure, or decrease our pain. Attachments to BEEPS help us medicate, and artificially regulate emotions in our brain. They take the place of secure attachments to God and healthy relationships with others. BEEPS are imposters in the brain and trick the brain into releasing dopamine. The dopamine generated from BEEPS is essentially a "weaker" form that provides instant reward, but not a lasting reward. On the flipside, this release of dopamine is more sought after than the long lasting pleasure that our brain was designed to "live in".

Entrope (en tro pay)- The Greek word for the emotion of shame. Also used as an island name. Shame is one of the Big Six negative emotions that we experience.

Capacity- (also see Joy Strength) This term describes the durability and strength of your bridge. There are many things that can affect your capacity. If a bridge is built with low levels of joy strength, then capacity will begin in a weak state. If a bridge suffers through a storm, then damage can be done to the capacity of even a previously strong bridge. See Appendix E, Chapter 3 for more detail.

Chara (Car uh)- Greek word for joy. (See joy for more explanation) Used as the name for the main island.

Eirene (I rey nay)- Greek word for peace, quietness, rest; the feeling of being whole and complete again. Similar to the Hebrew word shalom. See shalom for more details. Shalom is most often translated as peace.

Joy- To the brain, joy is the experience of knowing someone is glad to be with you. Communicated through eye contact, joy allows brain chemistry to match between people. See synchronization for more detail about how the brain chemistry matches between people.

Joy Strength- (also see Capacity) The amount of joy we have gathered to sustain us over time. For purposes of this book, we will consider Joy Strength on a scale of 1 to 10. If you have a Joy Strength level of 10, then you have a LOT of joy to help you maintain connections to God and others when you cross over into negative emotions. If you have a Joy Strength of one, then you can't easily maintain connection to God or others in the face of difficult emotions and you probably haven't had much experience of people being glad to be with you or haven't had the experience for a while. Joy Strength enables us to "build bridges". Without Joy Strength, our bridges will be weak and not able to withstand any storms that may come.

Lupe (loop ay)- The Greek word for the emotion of sadness. Also used as an island name. Sadness is one of the Big Six negative emotions that we experience.

Orgizo (Or gid zo)- The Greek word for the emotion of anger. Also used as an island name. Anger is one of the Big Six negative emotions that we experience.

Phobos (Fo bos)- The Greek word for the emotion of fear. Also used as an island name. Fear is one of the Big Six negative emotions that we experience.

Shalom- The experience of peace; such that everything is in the right amount, at the right time, in the right place. All is well with my soul, even if specific situations are not particularly happy.

Synchronization- The right hemisphere of the brain can communicate with the right hemisphere of the brain of another person through eye contact. During this period of non-verbal, eye-to-eye communication, the brains synchronize. If Person 1 is glad to be Person 2, then dopamine is released within the right hemisphere of Person 1, which is then duplicated inside the right hemisphere of Person 2. Another example of this occurs with negative emotions. If Person 1 is experiencing sadness, and Person 2 connects with them, again with eye to eye contact, Person 2 will also experience sadness momentarily. If Person 2 is able to maintain a state of being "glad to be with Person 1" while simultaneously experiencing sadness, then their "glad to be with you" state can draw the right hemisphere of Person 1 into synchronization with them and their 'joy' state - essentially "bridging them back to joy".

Pneuma (New ma)- Greek word for spirit, wind, or breath. This is just one of the names for the Holy Spirit. For the purposes of this story, I chose to use this word rather than the more common name of "Immanuel" often used in contexts of inner healing. Immanuel means "God with Us" and is another name for Jesus himself. Jesus left us with the Holy Spirit who can also be described as "God with us" and he said that having the Holy Spirit would be even better for us than having Jesus himself here in the flesh. The Pneuma is capable of guiding us, comforting us, counseling us, helping us, advocating for us and for all intents and purposes... building our bridges.

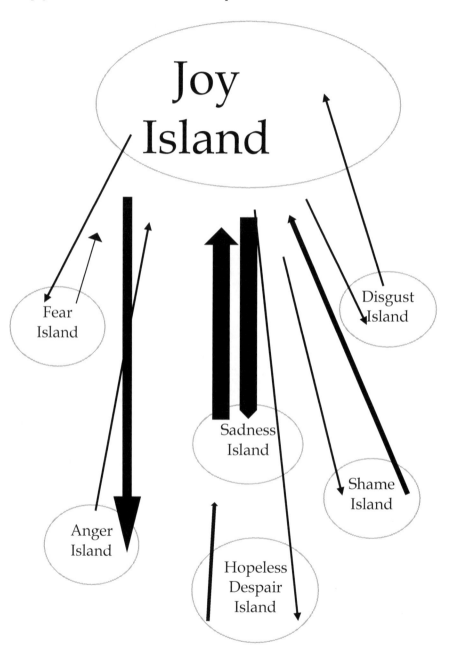

Appendix C: Eye Contact Journal

Day	Tick mark for # of times eye contact achieved	On a scale of 1-10 how would you rate your "joy strength" levels today overall?
Sunday		
Monday		
Tuesday		
Wednesday		
Thursday		
Friday		
Saturday		

*Even if the people in your household are sight impaired or have difficulty with eye contact, remember that there are opportunities to make eye contact everywhere you go!

Appendix D: Appreciation worksheets

Date:

Description of what I appreciated:

How it made me feel:

How it made my body feel:

What I did in response:

Short Name to help me remember this story in the future:

Date:

Description of what I appreciated:

How it made me feel:

How it made my body feel:

What I did in response:

Short Name to help me remember this story in the future:

Date:

Description of what I appreciated:

How it made me feel:

How it made my body feel:

What I did in response:

Short Name to help me remember this story in the future:

Date:

Description of what I appreciated:

How it made me feel:

How it made my body feel:

What I did in response:

Short Name to help me remember this story in the future:

Date:

Description of what I appreciated:

How it made me feel:

How it made my body feel:

What I did in response:

Short Name to help me remember this story in the future:

Appendix E: understanding the allegory

Chapter 1

Living on Chara: In the first two years of life, our brains are formed and designed to run on the chemicals produced by joyful experiences which are dopamine and serotonin. During joyful experiences where we experience someone being glad to be with us, the attachment center in the brain (level 1) tells the amygdala that life is good. The attachment center is responsible for informing the rest of our brain if proper levels of joy have been attained or not – whether we have experienced enough of 'people being glad to be with us' to establish the needed levels neurochemically. When the amygdala receives the message that this has happened it rests quietly. A quiet amygdala allows each of the other levels in the brain to do their jobs, functioning as they were designed to and a stable, joy-based identity capable of properly processing all emotions is created.

Joy is the response that takes place in your brain when you know that someone is glad to be with you. This happens at the subcortical level and is quicker than conscious thought. When you make eye contact with someone, your right orbital prefrontal cortex notices the right orbital prefrontal cortex signals that are being sent out from the other person. If that brain is glad to be with you, then dopamine is released in BOTH brains. This happens in six cycles every second.

Allowing rest/Recognizing Overwhelm: the brain requires rest when experiencing too much of anything, whether it is good or bad, pleasant or unpleasant. The brain recognizes that it needs rest and will send visible signals to those people he or she is interacting with, which indicate relief is needed. For example, at the beginning stages of overwhelm, one might avert eye contact or take a step backwards.

Once the brain of the other person receives those signals and rest is granted, then the brain has an opportunity to rest and recover so that it can reengage later. However, if they ignore those signals, we end up in a state of overwhelm. Sometimes, we even ignore our own signals and don't stop to rest when we need to. This also leads us into a state of overwhelm. This is when the brain sends signals to the amygdala that things are NOT GOOD. In fact, the continued release of stress hormones leads to "neuron death" and the "pruning" in the brain of necessary emotional connections. When the amygdala is in charge we no longer have access to the parts of the brain that contain important things like our identity, our logic, and our ability to access relational memories. Pushing past overwhelm on a regular basis, teaches your brain that resting is not allowed and perpetuates a cycle where overwhelm becomes your "normal".

The Bridges represent the neuropathways between the different parts of the brain that must be connected in order to maintain a healthy joyful identity with secure attachments. When situations occur that trigger an emotion, our brain assesses the information surrounding the event and emotion and tries to make sense of it. If it cannot, then the amygdala takes over and puts things on hold for processing. We need a neuropathway that runs from the appraisal center (or amygdala - level 2) all the way to the front part of our brain where our identity or sense of who we are is held (level 4). Principally, this is the neuropathway back to joy. This can only happen if someone is glad to be with us, assuring the amygdala that we will make sense of this together. When this has happened frequently, the amygdala approves that route more easily because it recognizes it as successfully well-traveled. Alternatively, without strong neuropathways running to the joyful identity center, the amygdala is more likely to choose a neuropathway that it has chosen before, such as staying in fear, anger, sadness, shame, or disgust. With good strong neuropathways in place, we maintain access to who we are and how it is like us to behave and can then make decisions based on that information rather than solely on the presenting emotional information in the immediate situation. Without these neuropathways, it feels like the emotions become louder than our identity.

Chapter 2

Living away from Chara: When the amygdala receives signals that life is bad or scary, then it takes control and runs our system on the chemicals that it produces. Those chemicals are adrenalin and cortisol. By design, adrenalin and cortisol help us to survive. That is their primary and only goal. They simply do not have what it takes to help your brain find happiness, contentment, relationships or anything other than survival. If we "live" this way then our identity forms in fear and all of our relationships and choices stem from the drive of "protection and survival". The brain recognizes this as a state of pain and, with the amygdala in charge, it lives in response to the perpetuating cycles of alarm that the amygdala generates. When our brain does not receive enough "glad to be with you" moments from those around us, the amygdala views life as bad or scary. When this happens, our brain becomes wired based on the fear driven system in the amygdala (level 2), or the kind of story the amygdala tells, instead of the joy driven system at level 1.

Negative Emotions: Our brain is designed to feel six different negative emotions, either singly or in some combination. These emotions are anger, fear, sadness, disgust, shame, and hopeless despair. During the first two years of life, the brain begins to develop neuropathways in the cingulate cortex (level 3) between those negative emotions and joy and quiet (levels 3 and 4). The cingulate cortex will only build these neuropathways if the amygdala is viewing life as good. As we build those neuropathways, and begin to experience a negative emotion, we have the opportunity to realize that our negative emotion is not permanent. At this point our brain alerts the amygdala that yes, life is still good even when we experience negative emotions, and then our amygdala doesn't notify the rest of our body that it's time to freak out.

Quiet side of joy: The brain functions best when it can flow rhythmically between high-energy states and low-energy states. When an infant smiles at her mother, dopamine is released and a high-energy state of joy is felt. When the infant has had enough, her eyes look away momentarily and the mother sees that it's time to quiet. This is when serotonin is released. Together they maintain a connection that allows for the quiet side of joy- or "shalom" (Eirene) to be felt. This is the moment when the brain feels safest, it knows that everything is in the right strength, the right amount and that it will not be pushed beyond its capacity to handle the high-energy states. The brain is made to cycle through this rhythm repeatedly and seeks to do this. The proper balance of dopamine and serotonin are present when this process is allowed to continue.

Chapter 3

Bridge Builder/ Bridge Master: This person is someone who has a stronger "brain" (with existing neuropathways) that can connect with others in order to help the less mature brain feel and match the chemistry of their own brain. During difficult events, the brain of the stronger person actually co-regulates the brain chemistry of the weaker person. This is typically the mother in the first 2 years of life. The bridge builder is able to synchronize and simultaneously feel the same negative emotion as the person they are glad to be with without becoming overwhelmed by it.

Bridge Owner: This person is currently experiencing a negative emotion in their brain because of something that happened to them. It is possible to experience a negative emotion without consciously being aware of it.

Impact of Frequency: In the brain, the neuropathways are established and kept based on the frequency of use. The more frequently one experiences negative emotions, the more established the connection to that emotion will be. The more frequently one can experience joy during a negative emotion; the more established the connection back to joy will be. Since joy is the experience of being "glad to be together", it can and does take place in the midst of a negative emotion. Returning to joy doesn't necessarily mean that the negative emotion is gone. Likewise, if one's "frequency" of use is minimal, the brain will naturally prune away that neuropathway since it sees it as non-essential. The brain has a "use it or lose it" philosophy. Sometimes we see "frequently used" and strong neuropathways built to one "default" negative emotion, like anger or fear whilst simultaneously a rejection of experiencing the other emotions is in evidence.

Tenderness toward weakness: When weakness is viewed as an opportunity to care, tenderness is the result. This is a critical ingredient for the development of the brain's identity center. When we display weaknesses and they are met with tenderness, we learn ways to grow and strengthen rather than ways to hide our weaknesses. In *Joy Starts Here*, a case for how crucial this tender response to weakness is can be found.

Synchronized brain chemistry: As mentioned in the "Bridge Builder/ Bridge Master" segment, it is not only possible, but very common for two brains to connect chemically. Another word for this process would be attunement. Attunement aligns states of mind between people who are in relationship and is communicated both verbally and non-verbally. This form of connection allows their feeling minds to resonate with each other and "feel felt". "Feeling felt" is a requirement for the brain to learn how to process its emotions.

Chapter 4

Storms represent trauma. Trauma can fall into one of two categories. Specifically, storms represent Trauma B which is the presence of "bad things" happening to us. When we experience Trauma B it overwhelms our capacity. If our capacity is small, like Eden's brand new bridge, then it doesn't take much trauma to destroy it. If we have a strong bridge, then we can withstand more trauma without losing our bridge. Trauma B can range from things like, abuse, death of a loved one, and rape to watching scary movies too young, being yelled at frequently, or losing your home to a fire or tornado. The amount of Trauma B we can handle is directly related to the size of our joyful connections. Trauma A is dealt with below

The Capacity & Strength of our bridge is a representation of two things. First, it indicates how much we have experienced Trauma A. Trauma A is the "absence of the good and necessary things in life". This would include things like malnutrition, homelessness, and not receiving love and appropriate touch as a child. The more Trauma A one has, the weaker their bridge would be because there are "holes" in their supply bucket. Building a bridge with a "dripping bucket" doesn't lead to a strong bridge. We can't build a strong bridge if all our "joy" leaks out of our bucket before we get a chance to build it.

This is exactly the problem with Trauma A. The bucket is a representation of capacity that has a direct correlation to how much weight our bridge can handle. The capacity and strength of our bridge is also directly related to how much joy we are receiving. Without joyful interactions with God or other people, then our supply bucket won't have what we need to build strong bridges.

Bridge Maintenance: The brain will prune away any existing neuropathways that it deems unnecessary. It prioritizes the pathways that are necessary based on how often they are used. The brain naturally goes through a large pruning period during adolescence.

Imposters and masks: Imposters are people who appear on the surface to be glad to be with us but don't really know who they are, let alone who we are. Imposters wear masks to protect themselves without realizing the dangers they pose. When we wear a mask, hiding our weaknesses, the brain knows that we are wearing a mask and will deflect any joyful "glad to be with you" messages with the logic that, "If they really knew who I was behind this mask, they would reject me". Masks essentially render all joy messages as null and void. Relationships with imposters also negate joy messages.

Eye Contact: The Right Orbital Prefrontal Cortex is located directly behind the eye. It receives signals that are brought in through eye contact for processing. Eye contact enables the brains of two people to communicate below the levels of consciousness. For example, during a joyful interaction between Bob and Jane, Bob is glad to be with Jane and dopamine is released in his brain. This causes him to smile. Jane's eyes see the smile, and notify her Right Orbital Prefrontal Cortex "Bob is glad to be with me" which then means dopamine is released in her brain as well causing her to smile. Bob's eyes pick up on Jane's smile and the cycle continues. This happens at six cycles **every second** for both Bob and Jane!

~*What about people that are blind?* Bonding and "glad to be with you" can also be generated through the other senses. In fact, infants utilize smell and touch primarily to experience "glad to be with you joy" long before sight comes on board! We also rely on taste and temperature regulation to help us bring in data that will communicate to us whether or not people are glad to be with us.

Default without joy: When the brain does not receive joy from the beginning, the attachment center at Level 1 does not form properly. This causes the amygdala to alert the rest of the brain that things are bad and scary. Without a well-developed attachment center, fear becomes the default setting for the brain. Fear drives all decisions, relationships and handles all emotions and when this happens, the brain eventually forms an identity based on fear.

BEEPS: See glossary

Chapter 5

Importance of comfort and validation: As we discussed earlier, it's very important for the brain to receive attunement during negative emotions. When we receive attunement we feel seen, heard, understood and we feel "felt". We know that someone is glad to be with us and that they care about us. When this happens, we can successfully navigate our way through even difficult life events that cause negative emotions. During attunement, we feel comforted by the presence of someone else, and we feel that our level of emotions is matched and validated. When this does not occur, we are more likely to be unable to fully process what has happened to cause us to feel a negative emotion, and as a result, the brain registers it as a traumatic event.

Relational Circuits/Brain's control center/Identity: Earlier in the story, we were made aware of three of the brain's five levels of control. Those levels were 1) Attachment Center 2) Amygdala and 3) Cingulate Cortex. In addition to housing your emotions, the cingulate cortex also contains some of the brain's Relational Circuitry. Level four, (the Right Orbital Prefrontal Cortex that we mentioned when discussing eye contact) holds the remaining Relational Circuits and is also considered the "Identity Center" of the brain. In order for Level 4 to be in working order, all the levels below it must be working properly and communicating that "life is good". These Relational Circuits (RCs) are what make it possible for us to relate to each other appropriately, receive joyful messages, retrieve relational memories, and stay aware of our identity. It is possible to begin to recognize when our RCs are not working properly and take steps to restore them. We want to do this so that we do not continue behaviors that aren't matched with our identity. When Level 4 is running efficiently, we "live on Chara".

Importance of joy building while repairing emotional systems: While undergoing "repair", the brain needs extra fuel to sustain function. Building joy- doing things that make you feel "glad to be together" allows the brain to "gather supplies" as well as rest and recover from focusing on painful things.

Power of Appreciation: There have been many studies done that have demonstrated that appreciation is good for relationships. Deliberately engaging in appreciation has been shown to stimulate a release of oxytocin, which prepares your brain for relational connections and bonding. Cognitive therapy research shows that deliberate appreciation is a very effective tool for producing positive emotions towards others and is a powerful key aspect in "happy marriages". In addition, appreciation of specific memories that are drawn from the experiential right hemisphere, rather than the abstract "title" of a memory in the left hemisphere, seem to have an increased effect. This right hemispheric engagement produces higher emotional intensity than the words alone.

Power of memory in the brain: Re-entering a memory and involving our right hemispheric recall of an event will automatically reproduce the same emotional responses of the original event. This is true in the case of "appreciation memories" and traumatic memories.

Chapter 6

Shared Capacity- Through attunement or synchronization, when we are connected to others we share the resources that their brain has for things like emotional capacity. We are then able to complete the emotional or maturational task at hand by borrowing some of their skills and resources. This is only possible when our Level 4 relational circuitry is on and in working order.

Breathing and the brain- The way that we breathe has a direct connection to our nervous system. When we are in a state of sympathetic arousal, our breathing rate increases and becomes more shallow. Inversely, when we are in a state of relaxation our breathing rate becomes slower, deeper, and a pause between respirations can be noted. These symptoms are automatic and we will do them without realizing it. The interesting thing is, we can take control of our breathing and send signals BACK to the brain about our environment. If we start breathing more slowly and deeply, the brain interprets that message as a notification that relaxation is in order.

We can use our body and the sensations our body has to change the functions of our brain.

Search for answers fear response- In order for our brain to determine whether a particular stimulus is dangerous to us or not, it must first "study" it. The evaluative circuits in the brain let us know if things are "good, bad or scary". Sometimes, the brain gets stuck trying to decipher all the input and a decision is delayed. When all attention is focused on evaluating if things are going to be hurtful to us or not, the brain sends out signals of arousal in preparation of a "bad or scary" result to its searches. This heightened feedback system reinforces the sensation of threat or impending doom. The reason for this is that the brain has deduced that when it can "make sense" of things, or "figure out cause and effect relationships" that it will be safer.

Science behind journaling: Journaling has been a tradition for centuries. Studies show that journaling can show a positive impact on your physical well-being, strengthen your immune system, and reduce the impact of stress on your physical health. Journaling engages both hemispheres of the brain- and using both hemispheres of your brain is a good thing! The left hemispheric use of words to explain your right hemispheric experience helps your brain tell a story that can be processed more fully in your memory. Once an emotional experience is fully processed into memory your brain is free to move on and won't waste valuable resources trying to make sense of it.

Biblical Concept: God's unlimited capacity: Scripture is full of examples of God maintaining who He is even in the midst of emotions that could have been overwhelming for most of us. In Ezekiel 20, you will find one of my favorite examples. This is just one of the times when God is repeatedly angered by the disobedience of the Israelites. Then God "thinks on his anger" and decides to choose to act like himself instead of just how he felt. In the New Testament we see Jesus, on the cross, enduring pain beyond anything we can imagine. However, he was still able to maintain access to his identity center, and act like himself. His brain did not become overwhelmed with the pain and did not shut down into solely amygdala responses. Even in His dying moments, his concern was for his mother and for the soldiers who took his life.

References

Friesen, Ph.D., J. G., Wilder, Ph.D., E. J., Bierling, M.A., A. M., Koepcke, M.A., R., & Poole, M.A., M. (2000). *Living from the Heart Jesus Gave You*. Pasadena, CA: Shepherd's House, Inc.

Hughes, D. A., & Baylin, J. (2012). *Brain Based Parenting: The Neuroscience of Caregiving for Healthy Attachment*. New York, NY: W. W. Norton & Company.

Karl Lehman, M. (2011, 2014). *Outsmarting Yourself: Catching Your Past Invading the Present and What to do about It Second Edition*. Libertyville, IL: This Joy! Books.

Khouri, E. (2007). *Restarting*. Pasadena, CA: Shepherd's House Inc.

Lewis, C. (1952). *The Chronicles of Narnia: Book Five: The Voyage of the Dawn Treader*. United Kingdom: Geoffrey Bles.

Maud Purcell, L. C. (2006, 12 12). *The Health Benefits of Journaling*. Retrieved 10 10, 2015, from Psych Central: http://psychcentral.com/lib/the-health-benefits-of-journaling/

Peter A. Levine, P. (2010). *In an Unspoken Voice: How the Body Releases Trauma and Restores Goodness*. Berkeley, CA: North Atlantic Books.

Siegel, D. J. (1999). *The Developing Mind*. New York, NY: The Guildord Press.

Wilder, E. J., Khouri, E. M., Coursey, C. M., & Sutton, S. D. (2013). *Joy Starts Here: the transformation zone*. East Peoria, IL: Shepherd's House Inc.

About the Author

 Denesia Christine Huttula or "Deni" as she's known to her friends lives in the foothills of North Carolina with her husband, two dogs, and a cat. Her two children are both grown and venturing forth in their own lives. A former photographer, with a bachelor's degree in psychology, Deni is now a Certified Life and Recovery Coach and works side by side with her father, Ed Khouri for his non-profit ministry: Equipping Hearts for the Harvest. Deni has an artist's and a therapist's heart and a Native American soul. When she's not working or writing, she spends her time exploring the nearby mountains. She has discovered great joy and peace in her relationship with Jesus after many difficulties in life and now has a calling to help others do the same. Visit her website www.theopenbench.com to get to know her even more.

Facebook: facebook.com/theopenbench

Twitter: @theopenbench

You can use this page as a bookmark and easy reference guide. Just cut along the line. ☺

The Bridges of Chara
Translation & Pronounciation

Chara (Car-uh)
JOY

Eirene (I-ray-nay)
PEACE

Orgizo (or-gid-zo)
ANGER

Apalegeo (ap-el-jay-o)
HOPELESS

Phobos (fo-bos)
FEAR

Anoia (I-u-nee-ah)
DISGUST

Entrope (en-tro-Pay)
SHAME

Lupe (loop-A)
SADNESS

Pneuma (new-ma)
SPIRIT, WIND, BREATH

Made in the USA
San Bernardino, CA
01 December 2016